AF444004

Twenty Minutes Away:

The Great War in the American Southwest

by Robert Stout

Prelude

Berlin - January 1911

"How fares the Kaiser?"

"Delusional, as always. He wants to incite another Moroccan crisis."

"And the Navy?"

"They're only willing to send a single gunboat. It's a compete was of time and coal!"

"Have you looked over von Schlieffen's notes?"

"Yes. They're interesting, but with the current strength of the army, wholly impractical. We would need an additional 400,000 trained troops. The economy could not take the strain"

"So we cannot press the French into a single, large confrontation?"

"No. Look at this map. Were we to invade Belgium, we could expect the British to join the Entente and stop or slow our advance here, around the Marne. We would outrun our supply lines and God knows what the result would be."

"Could we go through the Ardennes?"

"It's rough country, but perfect for hiding a large maneuver."

"We don't really have much rail capacity there. Could it be increased without alarming the French?"

"Probably, especially if we increase our raw lumber exports to Japan."

"We would have to undercut the American's price."

"I have an idea about that. What if we could get the Americans occupied with something closer to home?"

"Mexico?"

"They are unstable. Diaz announced that he would run again. The whole country is a powder keg."

"Would we support Diaz or the opposition?"

"Both, naturally. Open support for Diaz, arms and ammunition for the opposition, with the promise of full recognition to the winner."

"I'm sure Krupp would appreciate that, but how does it get the Americans off our back in Japan?"

"Any revolution in Mexico is bound to have unintended spillage into the border states. Taft would respond militarily and war would break out."

"If there were an organized government."

"We would need a President in Mexico strong enough to unite the country, but beholding to the ruling class. That would ensure enough instability to create the war"

"Someone who appears to be a reformer, but isn't?"

"I've got the perfect fool!"

"Who?"

"Francisco Madero He announced his run for the presidency and is garnering support."

"What makes him perfect?"

"He the son of wealth. His family owns an enormous amount of land in the north. I can't imagine that he would betray his own family by implementing land reform. He knows nothing of politics! We would have central stability and fringe instability."

"If Diaz falls, could we keep this Madero alive until the French and Russians attack us?"

"1916? I'm not sure. Five years is a long time to keep an angry people in check, even in the best of times."

"Can we advance the Entente's timetable for war?"

"Perhaps. We could leak Schlieffen's notes as a real plan and put, say, 1913, as our jump off date. Joffre would have to respond before we moved. That would give us two years to improve our rail access. Is that enough?"

"It should be. Who would we get to trigger the war between the United States and Mexico?"

"Does it matter? One of the peasants is bound to rise and we can steer them to our ends."

"And if Diaz doesn't fall?"

"The same scenario. His people hate him and his army. I imagine we could find someone along the northern border to ally with us."

"If Diaz wins, we would have more time for rail improvements, say until 1915."

"Are we sure the Americans would take the bait? They haven't been in a real war since the Mexican War. The war with Spain was a joke. Their own civil war barely lasted two months."

"Her army is small, but her resources are vast. Look at how fast the country responded to the Maine sinking. They immediately had more volunteers than they could handle.

We need only make the incident bloody enough. The

Americans will go to war."

"Are you sure the Japanese will buy the lumber?"

"Are you joking? After the Portsmouth Treaty, I'm

amazed that they even speak to the Americans. Can you

imagine? Winning a war against the largest country in the

world and then having the victory snatched away by

Roosevelt and Taft."

"I see your point. What about Roosevelt?"

"What do you mean? He's out of office."

"The threat of war is just the thing to get that cowboy

to run again. We could have Teddy in control."

"He wouldn't do it. It's against over 100 years of

precedence and remember what he did in the war with Spain.

He resigned from being Assistant Secretary of the Navy just

so he could be in the field in Cuba. The man has a death

wish."

"What about England? They have signed onto the

Entente."

"Secretly. If we keep out of Belgium until the French

invade it, any British support would cause their government to fall and we would look like heroes for defending Belgium."

"So we have the British and Americans put to the side. Our navy can run free from the North Sea with only the French to worry about. That leaves one large question open, Russia!"

"All their contracts to rebuild their navy are with us. I'm sure we can organize a work slowdown. As for their army, our spies say that they lack cohesive leadership and infrastructure in the First and Second armies."

"In plain language."

"Those two Imperial generals hate each other more than they do us. Cooperation between them is likely to be hesitant and poorly organized."

"That would buy us a little time, but they out number us two to one."

"They outnumber us only in manpower. They lack ammunition and a coordinated rail system. They can't get their men forward quick enough and, if they get to the front, they won't have enough bullets and shells to defeat us."

"What about the two wild cards, Italy and the Ottoman Empire?"

"The Italians would have to try to attack from the Alps. I can't see them breaking through. We can get the British to support the Turks if we can convince them that the Russians are violating the Anglo-Russian Convention."

"That would certainly divert the British. You think the Austrians can hold the Alps?"

"So long as they aren't pissing away their army against Russia, yes."

"And the Serbs?"

"The trick to the Serbs is to respond with proxies like Romania and Bulgaria. So long as Austria doesn't declare war, the Russians will hold off."

"You've given this a lot of thought."

"Five years, as soon as I heard of the French Plan XV. I've been modifying it as the details of Plan XVI have leaked."

"What is your time line?"

"By the end of this year, construction on the new Bavarian rail lines begin, Japan is approached about raw lumber sales, Mexico decides on Diaz or Madero. Early next year, assuming Diaz falls, war begins between Mexico and the United States, the Russians are implicated in a conspiracy in Persia, drawing the British away from the Entente. By the end of next year, Joffre receives the phony Schlieffen Plan. France attacks us along Alsace and Lorraine. We hold them, inflicting as many casualties on the French as possible. They respond by trying to flank us using Belgium, splitting their army. We hold at the Rhine and sweep through the Ardennes to destroy their armies in Alsace, then countermarch on Paris. It will be 1870 all over again, only this time, France cedes its territory north of the Seine!"

"Belgium, Holland, and Denmark become our protectorates! What about Russia?"

"I estimate two years of fighting without France will cause the moral to crumble. We infiltrate anarchists from exile and let them finish off the Russians for us."

"And America?"

"That war may never end."

Chapter 1

Waco, Texas - March 1916

Seventeen year old Jesse Washington looked out over the field in front of him. It had rained the night before and a thick Tule fog had formed, obscuring the view of the Mexican front line. As the sun began to rise, it became impossible to see an arm's length ahead and the fog became a brilliant white.

Jesse was a draftee When his number came up, he had reported just like all of the other colored men to the induction center. There, white officers evaluated the men for their suitability to become the latest cannon fodder in the Second Mexican War. Jesse was labeled 1-A and sent to Fort MacArthur for training. When San Antonio fell and the Mexican army moved northeast, training ended and he was given and old Krag rifle and put on the front line.

"Hey Jesse," a voice whispered.

"Quiet, I'm listening."

"Sarge says to check your receiver. Some of them are

cracked."

"Okay, now quiet," he hissed. Jesse listened intently. With such thick fog, his ears were his only means of detecting the enemy. There was a small crunch. It could be a Mexican or an armadillo. He wasn't sure It was dead quiet. Then, a thin sound pierced the morning calm. It was a bugle playing El toque a degüello. A few seconds later, the Mexicans, who had been advancing noiselessly broke through the fog with a chilling war cry.

Jesse managed four shots before the Krag's receiver jammed. He bayoneted a charging regular and took the soldier's Mauser. Unlike the Krag, the Mauser worked perfectly. Jesse dropped one man per shot until the rifle ran out of ammo. He worked the bayonet until the harsh scream of a bugle sounding retreat from behind.

In the thick fog and the confusion of war, Jesse was able to fall back to the second trench line. Gatling guns opened up and slowed the Mexican advance. The air was rank with the taste and smell of black powder. The white clouds of the guns and cannon only made the visibility worse. Jesse found a couple of dead Mexican soldiers and stripped them of their ammunition. He reloaded the Mauser with a stripper clip and turned to face the next advance.

They came out of the fog once again. There were no war cries this time, just the silent determination of the Mexican regulars. The second line broke without a shot being fired. What had been a retreat had turned into a rout. The draftees scattered, leaving their officers screaming orders for them to regroup. It did no good. The Mexicans took the final trench and advanced into Waco, killing every soldier they found on the way. Then, the fog broke.

Mexican sharpshooters had a field day. The dark blue uniforms of the Americans proved to be perfect targets for them. Artillery was unleashed at the remaining strong points and Waco fell to the Mexicans. The tri-color flew over Baylor University, or what was left of it.

Jesse ran, harder than he ever had before. Sniper's bullets licked at his feet as he wove in and out of cover. He still carried the Mauser. It gave him a false sense of security. As he broke from town, he headed to the only place he really knew, the Fryer's cotton farm.

"Missus Fryer! The Mexicans are coming!" he yelled.

"What are you talking about, Jesse?"

"The line south of town broke! They're killing everyone they find!"

"George! George!"

George Fryer came running up to the house. "What's this nigger doing here?" he asked angrily.

"Mistah Fryer, the Mexicans broke the line! They're killing everyone!" Jesse shouted.

"The lines broke? Where are the officers?"

"Dead, they're all dead! The Mexicans set up snipers in the fog!"

"Jesus! Lucy, throw some food and clothes into a hamper! Jesse, help me hitch up the wagon!"

Lucy returned inside and the men ran to the barn. Jesse led the horses out and George began to harness them. Lucy ran out of the house and threw a bag and a hamper into the wagon.

"Jesse, get in the back!" shouted George.

"No sir! I'll try and slow them here so you can escape!" replied Jesse.

"Don't be stupid! You're only one man!"

"They have cavalry! They'll stay to kill me if I make it hot enough for them! Get going!"

George whipped the horses and the wagon shot away. Jesse looked for a spot where he could pick off the advancing soldiers.

"The fallen tree!" he thought. "Just the place!" Jesse lay behind the tree and explored a cartridge box he had managed to grab from a dead soldier. Thirty rounds of the smokeless powder ammunition, 8mm Mauser. Jesse said a short prayer of thanks and reloaded the Mauser. The first of the cavalry showed, sweeping the fields for stragglers. Jesse aimed carefully and took out the third man in the line. The others spread apart, not sure where the fire had come from. His next shot rang out and the captain leading the detail fell from his horse, dead.

The Mexicans, leaderless and still unclear where the shots were coming from, spread out farther. A sergeant shouted orders. Jesse dropped him, too. The cavalry broke and rode hard back towards Waco. Jesse waited, then crept out into the field. He recovered two more cartridge boxes and caught one of the horses. He mounted the beast awkwardly, then managed to aim it north toward Fort Worth.

He kicked the horse and it took off running, with Jesse

barely hanging on.

Chapter 2

Fort Worth, Texas - March 1916

"What unit are you from, boy?" the sergeant barked.

"15th division, second battalion, company A." replied Jesse.

"And how is it you are on a Mexican officer's horse?"

"I caught it after I killed him and two others. Sergeant, the line at Waco has fallen!"

"Don't feed me that shit! We've had no word by telephone or telegraph from Waco! Are you a deserter, boy?"

"No sergeant, I ain't!"

"We'll see about that. You know anyone from Waco who could vouch for you?"

"Sergeant, all of the officers are dead! The Mexicans came out of the fog."

The sergeant looked around. The day was clear and warm. "The fog? In this weather?"

"It rained last night in Waco. Not much, but enough to raise a fog. The Mexicans have broken our line. They have seized Waco and are killing every bluecoat they come across!"

The sergeant looked over at a corporal and nodded. The corporal ran towards the signal office. He turned back to Jesse. "Why do you have a Mauser, boy?"

"My Krag jammed. I took this off a dead Mexican."

"And the ammo?"

"From the officer and men I killed at Fryer's farm, same place I got the horse,"

"I see." The corporal came running back to the sergeant. His face was white. He whispered in the sergeant's ear. The sergeant's eyes grew wide and he stood up. He pointed at Jesse, "Follow me!" They quick marched up to one of the wooden buildings. The sergeant wrote a hasty note and gave it to the soldier by the door. The soldier disappeared inside with the note.

"Who lives here?"

"Major General Greble. He'll want to talk to you."

The guard returned and ushered the two men in. They both saluted General Greble.

"Sergeant, you have intelligence for me from Waco?"

"Yes sir! This soldier is from the second battalion, sir!"

The general looked Jesse over with obvious distaste. "Deserter?"

"No sir!" Jesse replied.

The general hit Jesse across the mouth with a riding crop. "I wasn't talking to you, boy!"

Jesse's mouth began to bleed as he remained at attention.

"This soldier reported that the line at Waco has broken and Waco has fallen. The signal corps cannot get through to Waco, but towns north of there report a steady flow of single soldiers and civilians, sir."

"No organized units?"

"None reported, sir."

"Damn it! I need information I can act on. If they've forded the Brazos, they're only a day's ride from here!" He looked at Jesse, "Okay, boy, tell me exactly what you saw."

Jesse wiped his split lip. "Yesterday, in the morning, a dense fog rose around the trenches, sir."

"Gas?"

"No sir, a heavy fog. I was listening for movement when I heard a stick break. I tried to see into the fog and then a bugle sounded from the Mexican lines, sir."

"An order?"

"No sir. A kind of music, sir."

"Go on."

"They were on us immediately after the song started. They had used the fog to get close, then, over ran our trenches. I killed as many as I could, until my Krag jammed, then I picked up a Mauser and kept firing. Finally, I bayoneted a soldier who fell over me. By the time I got loose, the Mexicans had advanced past me. I picked up a cartridge box and scavenged ammo. Then I made my way back into Waco, sir."

"And what did you see there?"

"The officers sir. All dead in a row. I ain't ever seen anything like it, sir."

"Execution?" The general looked at the sergeant.

The sergeant nodded. "I believe they played the Degüello, sir."

"I see. Continue private."

"They had snipers in the taller buildings. They were picking us off each time we tried to reorganize. The men broke and I made my way up to Fryer's farm, sir."

"Why there?"

"I had worked for the Fryers and they always paid me on time. Didn't try to hold back on payin'. I wanted to warn them, sir."

"And did you?"

"Yes sir! I found Missus Fryer and she told her husband George. They hitched up a team and took off, sir."

"You didn't go with them?"

"No sir. I knew the Mexicans had cavalry and were looking for stragglers. If they found me with them, they would have killed us all, sir."

"I see."

"I setup behind a fallen log and waited for the cavalry troop. I shot the third in line so they wouldn't know where it came from. Then I picked off the officer and they began to mill around. Finally, I nailed the sergeant and they all took off. I waited, then gathered the spare ammo and caught the officer's horse. Then I came up here, sir."

"If you can ride, why weren't you placed in the cavalry?"

"It was my first time with a saddle, sir. Around the farm, we usually ride the plow horses bareback, sir."

"And you rode all the way from Waco?"

"I was too afraid to stop. If they caught me on an officer's horse, I was sure to catch it, sir."

"That will be all. Sergeant, give this man some food and deploy him to a cavalry regiment. I'll follow up with the orders."

Both men saluted and left. The guard came back in.

"Tell my officers that I expect them for dinner, tonight."

"Yes sir. Any regrets allowed, sir?"

"None."

Chapter 3

Forth Worth, Texas - April 1916

Jesse looked at his new billet. It was a barn converted for the black soldiers' use. He and about fifty others were tightly packed on the ground floor. The upper floor was still used for the horses' fodder. Jesse reported to the sergeant, a mountain of a man.

"Private Jesse Washington newly assigned to this company, reporting for duty."

The sergeant looked up, slowly. "You know how to ride?"

"A little."

The sergeant sighed. "Have you ever taken care of a horse?"

"Yes sergeant. I took care of the wagon horses we used on the farm."

"We'll start you slow. Corporal Beck!"

"Yes sergeant?"

"Take this new recruit over to the stables and have him muck them out."

"Yes sergeant." He turned to Jesse, "Come with me."

They walked to another large barn where the horses were stabled.

"Do you know how to muck out the stables?"

"Shovel out all the old straw and put clean straw in its place."

"Very good. The shovel is hanging over there. Start with this one and clean them all. I'll check in on you later."

"Yes corporal."

Jesse walked over to the wall and unhooked the shovel. He took it to the first stable. It wasn't too bad. Someone had cleaned the stable out within the last couple of days. He got a shovel full of soiled hay, then realized that he didn't know where he was supposed to put it. He set the shovel down and looked around the large barn. He found an old wheelbarrow, but he still could not find where it was being dumped. He dumped the waste into the wheelbarrow and laid in fresh straw. Another soldier walked into the barn.

"Excuse me!"

The soldier turned. It was a white officer.

"Oh, I'm sorry! Excuse me sir!" Jesse saluted.

"What is it?"

"I'm new and have been assigned to muck out the stable. Would you know where the waste is collected, sir?"

"There is a large pile about 500 yards due south. You may dump it there."

"Thank you, sir!"

"What's your name, son?"

"Private Jesse Washington, sir!"

"You aren't wearing a cavalry uniform."

"No sir. General Greble just assigned me."

"General Greble? Would you know why he's calling all his officers together tonight?"

"Yes sir. Waco has fallen, sir."

"How do you know this?"

"I was there, sir."

"Damn it! After you finish the stable, report to my barracks."

"Yes sir. Your name sir?"

"Major Pershing."

"Thank you sir. As soon as I have cleaned the stables."

Jesse spent the next three hours shoveling waste and spreading clean straw. Each time the wheelbarrow would fill, Jesse ran it over to an enormous pile south of the stable. As he was finishing, Corporal Beck returned.

"Good work. I'm sure the horses will be pleased. I have a new chore for you from the sergeant."

"I'm sorry corporal, Major Pershing has asked to see me."

"Black Jack Pershing?"

"I don't know. He told his name was Major Pershing."

"Damn boy, you don't waste any time, do you?"

"What do you mean?"

"Major Black Jack Pershing is the head of us buffalo soldiers. You didn't cross him, did you?"

"No. I think he wants to talk to me about Waco."

"Is that were you lived?"

"Yeah. Spent my whole life there."

"Well, you mind your manners around Major Pershing! You cross him and he'll make your life a living hell!"

"Thank you corporal."

"Call me Beck. Now, get over to the major's house and I'll tell the sergeant where you went."

Jesse jogged down to a row of neat houses. He walked up the street until he came to Major Pershing's residence. A guard stood out front.

"Private Washington to see Major Pershing."

The guard looked at him critically. "Boy, you smell like horse shit and you're filthy. Go around to the back porch!"

Jesse walked around the house to the back porch and knocked on the kitchen door. A black maid opened the door.

"Well, what do you want?"

"My apologies Ma'am. Private Washington to see Major Pershing."

"Boy, you stink. You stay right out here and I'll let the Major know you are here."

After a couple of uncomfortable minutes, Major Pershing showed up at the back door.

"Private, come inside!"

Jesse entered the neat house and followed the Major

into his library. In the middle was a table with a map of Texas opened on it. The Major reached down and pulled up a smaller map of Waco.

"Show me where you were deployed."

Jesse looked at the map. It was the first he had ever seen, but he soon realized that the blue line was the Brazos River. He ran his finger down the map. "We crossed here, then set up over here, sir."

It was south of Waco and used a line of hills to funnel the enemy towards the strongest trenches.

"You were in the forward trench?"

"Yes sir."

"How many trenches were behind you?"

"Three, sir."

"How did the Mexicans break through?"

"It was the fog. We had a light rain during the night and a thick fog formed, sir."

"How far could you see?"

"When they came? About arm's length in front of me was all, sir."

"Did they use the cavalry to break the line?"

"No sir. It was their army. The cavalry mopped up strays."

"Did you engaged the Mexicans?"

"Yes sir. I fired until my Krag jammed, then picked up a Mauser and kept shooting.

Pershing frowned. He had heard that the new black troops were given the old Krags, but until now he hadn't any proof. He closed his eyes and pictured the battle. Heavy fog covering the Mexican approach, men with obsolete rifles, unaware until the Mexicans were on them. It would have been a rout.

"Was there any attempt to retreat?"

"Retreat sounded, but it was too late, sir. The Mexicans had overrun all four trenches."

"How did you get up here?"

"I sniped three cavalry men, took the best horse, and rode north, sir."

"What about reforming with your officers?"

"They were all dead, sir. The Mexicans shot them against a wall."

"What kind of weapons did their cavalry use?"

"Mausers, sabers, and the officer had this." He handed Pershing a Luger. "They were pretty heavy with ammunition, sir."

"How heavy?"

"They each had over 200 rounds of rifle, sir."

"Rations?"

"Looked to be three days only, sir."

Pershing let out a breath. "They aren't going to move but they are going to secure Waco."

"Sir?"

"Not enough rations to get them to Fort Worth, but enough ammo to keep us out of Waco for a while."

Pershing turned back to the map. "Can you read this?"

"Barely. I recognized the river bend, sir."

"These are buildings, this is hills, and the blue is water."

"Yes sir."

"How could a man get back into Waco without being seen?"

"Here, sir." Jesse pointed at the map. "This is where the old Underground Railroad was, in these hills."

"Thank you Private Washington. I will remember your

assistance." Pershing wrote a quick note and handed it to

Jesse. "Give this to your sergeant." he saluted and Jesse

returned the salute. Jesse made his way out to the back

porch, then back to his sergeant's station.

"A note from Major Pershing, sergeant."

The sergeant took the note and read it slowly.

"You know what this says?"

"No sergeant."

"Go get clean, then report back to me."

Jesse walked toward the showers and wondered just what the

note had said.

Chapter 4

General Greble's House, Fort Worth, Texas - April 1916

General Greble addressed his officers. "Gentlemen, I have just informed President Taft of the loss of the city of Waco to the Mexicans."

There was an audible gasp from most of the officers.

"The President would like us to get it back, of course, with all due haste, but we also have to protect northern Texas. I'm open to suggestions."

"Envelopment and cutoff from reinforcement and supplies," offered Colonel Cabell.

"Our enveloping units could just as easily be enveloped themselves," replied Colonel Read. "We are stretched as it is with the loss of Santa Fe."

Greble turned to Major Pershing, "Do you have an alternate plan?"

"Yes sir. We don't know enough about the Mexican deployment to make an educated decision. Are they entrenched south of the Brazos or at the cities northern outskirts? How large was the force of invading troops? We have a new recruit who is intimately familiar with the territory around Waco. We could send in a few men to act as our eyes and ears, getting a full accounting of the Mexican strength and deployment."

"Your buffalo soldiers?" asked Colonel Read.

"Precisely. No one is going to pay attention to a few Negro civilians. I would give them, say, a week, and we should have our intelligence."

"I don't like it," said Colonel Cabell. "The Negro troops folded at Waco."

"The Negro troops were given obsolete Krags in Waco. We know from our own experience that the rifles jam when given the newer ammunition," replied Pershing. "They never really had a chance."

"And you would give them that chance?" asked Greble.

"Yes, general, I would. I've worked with them for over twenty years. I know just how good they could be if they were given a chance."

"Are there any other objections to Major Pershing's

plan?"

"Would you arm them with the new Springfields?" asked Cabell. "I'm not sure we want to arm our Negro forces so near the south."

"They would have to be unarmed," explained Pershing. "Anything, a pistol or a knife, would give them away. Unarmed and in civilian clothes."

"They could be shot as spies," Read pointed out.

"I know. Ideally we would be able to launch an expeditionary force to retake south Texas, as Colonel Cabell suggested, but we do not have enough trained men and officers. With the men we have, we will need to know exactly where we can strike."

General Greble stood. "Gentlemen, it seems Major Pershing's plan is our best option. Major, select your men and send them in. We need that information!"

The officers stood, saluted General Greble, then filed out of the dining room. Major Pershing stayed behind.

Greble looked at Pershing, "Jack, if you can pull this off, I'll make you a lieutenant colonel."

"Thank you sir!"

"Don't thank me yet. If your troops do not perform, you'll be busted back to captain. Now, what do you need from me?"

"A couple of good horses for the spies to ride down to Waco. They'll dismount north of town and I'll bring the horses back. Then meet with them again in a week's time."

"Do you have to go?"

"My officers are too green. Even if they could get there and back, I doubt that they could make the rendezvous a week later. Any news from Europe?"

"The French have invaded Belgium. The Brits are giving them three days to withdraw."

"And the Germans?"

"Still holding off the French in Lorraine."

"Why haven't they counterattacked?"

"Nobody knows. The bulk of the German army has disappeared. The men in Lorraine are only a small part of their forces. Additional units have beefed up the Rhine and the Russian front, but not enough to account for all of them."

"The Ardennes. It's the only place they could be."

"It's all heavy forest. An army could barely move

there."

"Perfect place to hide them. I'll bet the counterattack comes out of there, flanking the French army at Lorraine."

"What about the Rhine?"

"Hold the French or blow the bridges. The counterattack could cut the French off from the army at Lorraine."

"Exposing Paris!"

"I had a look at that Luger the private picked up in Waco."

"And?"

"It was made in Connecticut for Luger of Germany."

"You think they're reselling the arms they buy from us to our enemy?"

"I think so, yes. The question is, why?"

Chapter 5

Near Waco, Texas - April 1916

"This is as far as you go. From here on out you walk. Meet me back here in seven days' time. If one of you doesn't make it, I'll assume the Mexicans killed you. Understood?"

"Yes Major Pershing!"

Pershing took the reins of the two horses and began galloping back to Fort Worth. Corporal Beck looked at Jesse.

"If you get me killed, I'll never forgive you!"

"Just stick with me and do what I do and you'll be fine."

"Great, which way?"

"We head east to the Brazos, then follow it south into Waco."

"And which way is east?"

"It's afternoon, so away from your shadow."

'What do you think we'll find?"

"Mexicans, and maybe what they're up to."

"You know, I'm just a cavalry man. What did you ask

for me?"

Jesse laughed, "Yours was the only name I knew!"

Near dark, they approached the Brazos.

"Lay your quilt here. It's far enough from the river we won't get bit too bad by the skeeters."

They laid out their rolls and looked to the south.

"Is that light down yonder Waco?"

"I think it's a fire. Too big to be Waco."

"Do you think they're burning the city down?"

"Maybe. We won't know until tomorrow. Get some sleep."

Beck stared at the stars and thought about his home in Tennessee. It wasn't much, just a shack, really. However, it managed to keep him dry in the rain and the bugs off him in the heat. He fell asleep wishing that he was in that little shack.

Jesse rested, but he didn't sleep. The last time he saw Waco, it was splattered with the blood of his friends and fellow soldiers. Now, the big light implied something worse was underway. He missed his rifle and prayed they wouldn't be caught by the scouts, or worse, some Comanche out of

Comancheria. At least he could talk his way past the scouts. The Comanche, he had been told by his mammy, took no prisoners and never let anyone go. Better to die by a Mexican bullet.

Just before dawn, Jessie woke Beck up.

"Time to move. Get your stuff and be real quiet."

Beck packed his roll.

"Not like that! They'll spot you as a soldier for sure!"

Jessie unwrapped Beck's roll and threw it together in a much sloppier fashion.

"Here. You wear it like this. And keep your head down. You don't look nobody in the eye, you hear me?"

"Got it. What about how I speak?"

"Just listen and try not to speak much. Probably will save us both."

They made their way south, walking across the rich farmland southwest of the Brazos. Around noon, they came to a Mexican guard post.

"Your papers, please!" barked the sentry. It was a please that was anything but a polite request.

"We ain't got's none. Me and Beck heard there was

jobs don here for black folk."

The sentry, apparently at the end of his English fluency, called for an officer. The officer came out of the small building. He put on a pair of pince-nez glasses and walked over to the two black men.

"My guard says that you two are looking for work? We'll see." He motioned to the guard who took their rolls and spread them out. He felt the quilts for any hidden papers or unexplained bulk, then nodded to his commander.

"Who are you?"

"My name is Jessie and this is my cousin Beck."

"And why do you want to work for us?"

"We heard you paid in silver and don't care that we are black."

"You information is correct. Do you know the area?"

"No suh. We be both from Tennessee."

The officer nodded to the guard. The guard searched them and only found a few pennies.

"What was your last job?"

"We wuz workin' on my uncle's place helping him with sharecropping a field of tobacco."

"We aren't growing tobacco here."

"And we wasn't gettin' paid."

The officer smiled and took off his glasses. "Can you two handle shovels?"

"Yes suh, we can."

"Very well." He withdrew a paper from his tunic and wrote on it. "This will get you into the water project. Work hard and keep a low profile. You'll be paid every Friday in silver pesos. The guard will point you in the right direction."

'Suh?"

"Yes?"

"What about them papers the guard wants?"

"You'll get them at the project. Anything else?"

"No suh and thank you suh!"

The officer shook his head, then walked back into the building. The guard pointed due west and the pair began to walk again.

Beck looked at Jessie. "You don't speak that way!"

Jessie smiled, "First time in the deep south?"

"Yeah. I'm from Chicago."

"Learn to speak that way. Play stupid and a little lazy.

You may get beat a little, but you won't be found out. We only have to do this dog and pony show for a week."

'Yes suh, mista Jessie."

"Maybe we can say you were hit in the head as a child and can't speak much!"

"Right. What do you think the project is?"

"I don't know. No one was building anything before the fall."

Eventually, they saw some more buildings. Again, they were stopped by a guard.

"Papers!"

Jessie handed the man the paper that they had received from the officer. The guard read it, then waved them past.

"I'm sorry, where do we go now?"

"Por ahí, pendejo." He pointed to the red building.

They walked into the building and, at a desk, sat George Fryer.

"Good afternoon, Mister Fryer."

Fryer looked up. "You aren't wearing blue."

"No sir. It wasn't good for my health."

Fryer smiled a little. "What do you need?"

"Just some work for me and my cousin."

'His name?"

"Beck. He doesn't speak much, but he's a hard worker."

"That's good. I doubt the Mexicans could understand him, anyway. We're digging a ditch. Can he shovel?"

"We both can, sir."

"The Mexicans have dug out the bulk of it using steam shovels, but want men to finish it by hand."

"A ditch?"

"A canal. Let me see your papers."

Jessie offered the papers to George.

"Do you read Spanish?"

"No sir."

"This says you and your cousin are spies and that you should be executed upon arrival here."

"We ain't spies!"

"I didn't say you were. The commander at the guardhouse did." He withdrew two papers from his desk and began to write on them. "These are your new work papers.

They're good until you leave this area or the commander

checks on you two, whichever comes first." He looked at

Jessie square in the eye and lowered his voice. "Lucy wasn't

as lucky as me. Consider this full payment for trying."

"Thank you Mister Fryer."

"Go to the green building and they'll outfit you two."

"Yes sir!"

Chapter 6

McLennan County, Texas - April 1916

The canal was deep, maybe twenty feet, and bone dry. Men lined the bottom and squared off the sides with shovels. The men were nervous and finally, a peon broke from his work and began to shout in Spanish.

"Van a inundar el canal y nos matan a todos!"

A shot rang out from the guards and the man dropped. A guard walked up to the wounded man and shot him in the head.

A voice came from the canal's top. "You work for us because we pay you and feed you. Any attempts to slow or disrupt our work will be met with a bullet! Comprendemos?"

"Si!" rang out from the workers. They kept shoveling.

When the sun finally began to set, the men were offered ladders from the top and they began to climb out of the canal. They lined up and took metal plates, then walked the food line. Today, as always, were rice and beans with some tortillas.

Jessie and Beck sat down by an oak tree.

"We get paid, tomorrow."

"If we survive."

You think they mean to kill us?"

"I don't think they care one way or another, so long as the canal is finished."

"Our hand work is pretty well complete. What will they do next?"

"Blow the plugs at each end and flood the canal."

"Each end?"

"The Brazos and Hog Creek. It'll protect Waco on three sides."

"Explains the rush to get it done."

"What was that guy yelling about before they shot him?"

"I don't know. I heard the word canal and todos, which means all."

"I think it's time we left."

"I agree. Any idea how?"

"I would say tonight, but now that they shot that guy,

they'll be on guard."

"Maybe to the south. Deeper into Waco itself."

"You crazy?"

"A little. If we get south of town, we can cross the South Bosque then head to our rendezvous."

"I can't swim."

"Neither can I. The South Bosque isn't that deep, at least until they open the canal."

"Then what?"

"It'll flood all the way to Hog Creek. Rivers to the north and east, a swamp to the west."

"We aren't going to recapture Waco, are we?"

"I don't see how. Better to get San Antonio and starve them out of Waco."

"Tomorrow we get paid."

"So?"

"Freshly paid miners will want to blow their money. No one would stop us if we were found in the red light district and near the cantinas."

"The canal could be open by then."

"If it is, we're out of luck anyway. There will be no

way back to Major Pershing."

"If you wanted to go tonight, what would be the easiest way?"

"Lower a ladder into the canal, then use the same ladder to scale the other side."

"And what would be the craziest way?"

"Go down to the heavily guarded ends and walk across the plug."

"Somebody is bound to try to cross tonight."

"And will use the ladders."

"If you were a guard and saw a ladder fallen in the canal, what would you do?"

"Sound the alarm and begin to search for the escaping workers."

"And if you couldn't find them?"

"Get as many guards as I could to search the canal."

"Taking them away from the nearest plug?"

"Naturally!"

"How much time would it give us?"

"Maybe twenty minutes until they figure out no one is down there."

"I will need a bottle of tequila."

"Why?"

"It'll let me get close to the remaining guards."

"That rummy Miller has one."

"Can you get it?"

"Can we take him with us?"

"Only as far as the canal."

"If he doesn't know that..."

"Get the bottle. We'll leave just after midnight."

Chapter 7

McLennan County, Texas - May 1st, 1916

As the drunk staggered up towards his post, the guard

yelled out, "Alto!" The drunk smiled and held up a

bottle of tequila. Then he clumsily put his finger to

his lips and said, "Shhh."

The guard relaxed a little and the drunk staggered up

to him and handed him the bottle. The soldier took the bottle

and sipped, never taking his eyes off the drunk. The drunk

motioned for him to take a large slug. The guard threw back

his head and took a large mouthful of tequila. The drunk

quickly reached over and withdrew the bayonet from the

guard's belt and cut the guard's throat. He caught the bottle as

the guard dropped.

Beck signaled for Jessie and Miller to join him. "Two

more. No shooting." Jessie picked up the rifle and put on the

helmet, standing where the guard had been stationed. Beck

began to stagger up the road to the next guard.

The guard looked down at Jessie and received a thumbs up. He eagerly took the bottle and soon lay dead at Beck's feet. Beck motioned for the two others to advance. "There's a fourth, manning the carbon lamp. We need a quiet distraction. Miller, get some rocks from the plugs edge!"

Miller did as he was told. He didn't trust Negroes, but these two had been square with him. As he leaned down, Beck kicked him over the side. Miller never even yelled, just looked surprised. He hit the bottom with a large thump and began to moan. Beck signaled the last guard to come over and the carbon light illuminated the canal. The guard at the light focused on the broken Miller. Jessie came up from behind and slit his throat. The guard whom Beck had signaled for was looking in the canal as Beck pushed him in. The guard impaled himself on his own gun when he hit the bottom. Now armed with a Mauser, a bayonet, and a box of bullets each, Jessie and Beck crossed the plug and disappeared into the night.

At dawn, they heard the sound of muffled explosions to their south.

"Plugs are opened."

"Keep hiking north. I don't want to get stuck in a swamp."

Beck grunted and they continued the long walk. Around ten, they spotted a rider on the horizon with two extra horses.

"It's the major!" shouted Beck.

"Something's wrong. He should be farther north."

"Maybe we just made good time."

"Maybe. Keep a low profile just the same."

They began to close the distance, crouched low to the ground. The figure sat there. The two tethered horses moved around.

"His horse isn't moving."

"What?"

"Watch his horse."

The two men stopped and watched the horses. The two empty horses were peacefully grazing. The third horse kept its head up and didn't move.

"Do they know we're here?"

"I don't think so. They know how we work, so this would be a natural trap."

"Let's go wide. We can come back if we don't find the major!"

They made their way due west until they could no longer see the horses. Then they began to hike north again. At dusk, they saw another set of three horses. They watched for a while and realized that this, too, was a trap. Again, they made their way west, then turned north. After sundown, they lay in the rough and tried to get some sleep.

"Beck?"

"Yeah?"

"The major isn't due until tomorrow."

"Where do you suppose the Mexicans were?"

"Off in the brush near the horses. Close enough to see and shoot, but far enough that we

If we catch them unaware, we can steal their horses."

"Maybe, but they could have doubled up, making four shooters."

"You may be right. After last night, I don't think they'll ever underestimate us again."

"Pity about Miller, though."

"Can you imagine him out here? He would have run

straight to the horses and gotten us all killed."

"Still, we did use his tequila."

"Yeah. The look in his eyes when I booted him off. So surprised he didn't say a word."

"Yeah, but a rummy is a rummy. You can't take a wet head out here and just leave him. Killing him was a kindness."

"Still..."

"Yeah."

They slept fitfully until just before dawn. When the sun broke, they took their bearing and headed northeast. After a few hours, they stopped and rested.

"What do you think?"

"We're too far north, but I haven't seen his tracks."

"Me either. Let's start due east."

At noon, they spotted a rider with three horses. They watched for a bit and realized it yet another trap.

"Now what?"

"North."

Gradually, as the two continued north, a tower began to appear on the horizon. As they drew near, it became a clock tower atop a large courthouse.

"We're way too far north. That's the Meridian courthouse!"

"Damn it. Do they have sundown laws?"

"I don't know. They should have a telegraph, though."

They walked into town and followed the wires to the telegraph office.

"Howdy, how can I help you two?"

"We need to send a telegram to Fort Worth, but we're broke."

"Are you in the service?"

"Yes sir, we are."

He slid them a piece of paper. Write your message here and I'll send it to the commander of the post."

"Thank you. Are there sundown laws here?"

"No sir. We are free of such nonsense in Meridian."

Jesse slid the operator the note.

"Let's see, Washington and Beckley in Meridian Stop Notify Major Stop Awaiting orders. Stop. Is that it?"

"Yes sir."

"You boys have a seat and I'll send it off."

"Thank you. Is Fort Worth the nearest army base?"

"That it is. A good three-day walk over and up the Shawnee Trail, if you have water."

They sat on the bench and the telegraph operator sent their message. It was answered almost immediately.

"Says here target status? Stop. What the hell does that mean?"

Beck took a pencil up and wrote a new message. "Here, send this."

"Protected three sides Stop Suggest San Antonio first Stop."

"Is that it?"

"Yes sir. If you would."

The new message was sent. They didn't have to wait long for a reply.

"Understood Stop Arrange quarters with rangers Stop Major will meet you there Stop Greble Stop"

"Looks like you two are going to be here awhile. The ranger station is just down the street."

The two tired soldiers got up and made their way

down to the Texas Ranger's office. Behind a desk sat a man dressed in normal street attire.

"May I help you boys?" he asked.

"Yes sir. Are you the Captain here?"

The man chuckled. "Nope, Sergeant Carnes at your service."

"I'm Corporal Beckley and this is Private Washington." He handed the telegram to the sergeant.

He read the telegram carefully. "Who's Greble?"

"Major General Greble is the commandant of Fort Worth."

"That explains why I don't know him, I usually work south and west. Well, you boys need accommodations and you got your choice. You can have a pair of bunks in the jail or can sleep in the barn."

"Are the bunks ticky?"

"Most certainly. Bed bugs, too."

"We'd be honored to take the barn."

"Smart choice. Just fleas out there. You'll both need to surrender your rifles for the length of time you're in Meridian, but you can keep the bayonets."

The two soldiers handed the rifles to Sergeant Carnes. He looked at the fabrication mark.

"These were made in the US," he stated flatly. "Since when are Model 98's made in Connecticut?"

"We got them from the Mexicans."

"The Mexican army?"

"Yes."

"The Germans are buying US built guns and selling them to the Mexicans?"

"It would appear so."

"Damned if our own greed isn't going to kill us all! You two need some rest. The barn is out back. I'll call you in for dinner."

Chapter 8

El Paso, Texas - May, 1920

Colonel Pershing stared through his field glasses across the Rio Grande. It was clear that the Mexican army was gathering at Ciudad Juárez . The gains of the previous year had been tough and had cost many lives, but the Mexicans were cleared from most of Texas, being held to south of the Nueces River. Now the Mexican army seemed to be gathering to re-invade El Paso, for the third time in the war.

"Lieutenant Washington!"

"Yes, Colonel!"

"Tell Captain Beckley to expect probing missions tonight and a full attack tomorrow. We can't let the Mexicans set the time for the battle."

"Yes Colonel!"

Jessie turned and rode down towards the Rio Grande, where Beck had his men emplaced. He found him reviewing the trenches which cut through the middle of El Paso.

"Captain Beckley!"

The captain turned his horse around and rode over to Jessie.

"What is it, Jess?"

"The old man wants probing missions tonight and a full attack in the morning."

Beck shrugged, "With what? Tell the Colonel that the influenza has dropped me down to thirty percent strength, with the rest either dead or dying."

"Is that true?"

"I'm afraid so. If those Mexicans decide to retake El Paso, it won't be much of a fight."

"Any sign of the influenza across the border?"

"Nope. They either don't have it or are making sure we don't know that they have it."

"Can you do an infiltration and bring back a few prisoners?"

"Sure. Is that what the Colonel wants?"

"Keep inspecting. I'll tell him what you told me."

Jessie rode back up the gentle slope towards Fort

Bliss, then looked back. Most of El Paso was a smoking ruin. A city that would normally be bustling with international trade was deserted with most of its buildings still ablaze from the last attempt of the Mexicans to take the city. Pershing was waiting for him atop the crest.

"Well?"

"Captain Beckley reports that he is down to thirty percent effective, with the influenza accounting for the rest."

Pershing looked at Jessie. "Do you think he's lying?"

"A little. I would estimate nearer to forty percent effective, but that still isn't enough to dislodge the Mexicans."

"Suggestions."

"I would have Beckley's scouts infiltrate and capture some of the Mexicans. We have no intelligence on whether or not they are effected by the influenza."

"Make it so. I have a telegram from the capitol."

"Yes sir?"

"The influenza has taken over half of the country's population. There will be no reinforcements. What we have is it."

"It's not enough to take them, sir."

"I would be happier if the battles weren't so glorious and the Mexicans didn't fight so well. At our current rate of attrition, they'll be able to walk across the entire Southwest without seeing a single soldier."

"Is there anything we can do?"

"The British have captured a French infernal machine used to cross the trenches. It has tractor tracks and a cannon on a turret on top, like a battleship. Maybe technology can stop this war."

"What about the Germans?"

"Stopped east of Paris at the Seine. They can't seem to coordinate with the British attacks. I don't think they anticipated Italy's support for France, either. Over a million Italians have been deployed to France. They're devastating the German army's southern flank."

"And Russia?"

"Good news from there. Kerensky's troops have pushed the Germans back to the Oder River. Lenin and his supporters have been tried for treason and executed. The Mensheviks are in control."

"This seems like it will never end. It's all so hopeless."

"Cheer up, Lieutenant. Seven years ago when this war started, a black man could never be an officer. Now, half of my staff are Negroes. Segregation is dead and we've proven the value of the black man."

"Yes sir, but the cost. Between the war and the flu, we've lost half our population."

"So have most of the countries in the world. War is never a pretty thing, Lieutenant, especially when it catches you unawares like this one did us. But, occasionally, it provides the boost people need to do the right thing."

Chapter 8

Ciudad Juárez, Mexico - May, 1920

At nightfall, Beck rode with a handful of men to the west, then followed the foothills south, to the Samalayuca Dune Fields. They dismounted and staked their horses in the dunes, then proceeded on foot towards the southern part of Ciudad Juárez. Silently, they slipped along the buildings, searching for soldiers to kidnap. At a small house, they spotted two officers mounts tied to a tree. They carefully scouted the building and determined it was just the two officers and the cook. They waited until the cook retired and the two men sat out on the veranda to smoke their cigars. The two officers sipped brandy as they smoked and moved gently in their rocking chairs.

"Ramon, ¿crees que los estadounidenses saben lo débiles que somos en el frente?"

"Es improbable el coronel. Hemos mantenido a los enfermos a cubierto desde que comenzó la maldita gripe."

Beck breathed softly. The Mexicans had the flu! He waited and listened more.

"¿Qué dicen los alemanes?"

"Están cortando nuestros envíos de armas. Al parecer, los necesitan en Francia".

"¡Esos imbéciles! ¿Cuándo saldrá en línea la fábrica de Mauser en Tehuacán?"

"No mucho. El problema es la fábrica de municiones en Puebla. Las balas están saliendo, pero tienen problemas con la artillería. Los proyectiles no son lo suficientemente confiables para usarlos".

Beck signaled his men. They advanced silently toward the patio, using the cactus as cover. As both officers tipped back their brandy, the soldiers ran and held pistols to the officers' heads.

"¡Silencio! ¡Ven con nosotros! ¡Intenta escapar y estás muerto!" hissed Beck. The two officers, handcuffed and gagged, were silently led out of town. When they reached the dunes, Beck's men recovered their horses and escorted the prisoners north to El Paso.

The troop arrived back in El Paso about dawn.

Waiting for them were Colonel Pershing and Lieutenant Washington.

"Captain Beckley! Nice work. You and your troop have the morning off," shouted Colonel Pershing. "Lieutenant, bring to me one at a time!" Pershing turned and walked back into his office. Beckley left one officer with Jesse and had his men escort the other to the lock up. Pershing's guard escorted the other into the office.

"Jesse, the pair were talking about the influenza when we captured them."

"And?"

"That's all I could make out. Oh yeah, something else about Mausers."

"Thank you Beck. Where did you get them?"

"South side of town. They were enjoying drinks on the porch."

"Bring any back?"

"No time to. I'm just happy we got them."

"We'll take what we can get. Were you able to infiltrate cleanly?"

"Slick as a whistle. Their guards were few and far

between."

"Any papers?"

"Nah."

"Think they'll talk?"

"No. They're both officers."

The guard came outside. "You two. The Colonel wants to see you!"

They went into the office. The Mexican was seated in a chair, perspiring heavily. Colonel Pershing handed him a glass of water.

"He has the influenza," Pershing said matter-of-factly. "I doubt if he will live the day."

"Was he any help?"

"A little. He confirmed they, too, have the flu. Take him to the infirmary and bring the other one in."

They both saluted, then carefully got the Mexican to his feet. They walked him out and over to the infirmary, placed him on a bed, then cuffed him to the cast iron headboard. Beck informed the head nurse about their new patient, then he and Jesse walked over to the lock up. The guard challenged them.

"Halt and identify!"

"Captain Beckley and Lieutenant Washington."

"You may pass."

"What cell did you put the Mexican in?"

"Cell one. It was empty."

"It had ten prisoners yesterday."

"The influenza, sir."

They opened the door and took the Mexican Colonel to Colonel Pershing's office.

Pershing looked at his Mexican counterpart and said to Captain Beckley, "You are dismissed. Washington, stay."

Captain Beckley returned to his men. Colonel Pershing began the questioning.

"Do you speak English?"

"Si, a little."

"What is your name and rank?"

"José Doroteo Arango Arámbula, Ejército Mexicano, Teniente coronel."

"You are dying, Colonel."

"Si, la Gripe."

"Do you have any family left to notify?"

"No, todos muertos."

"My condolences."

"Gracias. ¿Puede ayudar a mi Capitán?"

"I can."

"Tiene una esposa e hijo en Ciudad Juárez." The man began to make a horrible, rasping noise.

"Colonel, is your captain sick, too?"

Jesse wondered what the Colonel was up to. He knew perfectly well the captain was ill.

"Todos están enfermos. Hasta los doctores están enfermos."

"I see. Do you have Germans in your camp?"

"No, los alemanes se fueron cuando llegó la gripe."

"Washington, assemble the troops."

"Yes sir!" Jesse turned and left the two alone.

"We will take Ciudad Juárez. Do you wish to be buried there?"

"Si, gracias coronel." The man wheezed once more, then made a final exhale and died.

Chapter 9

Mexico City, Mexico - September 1923

The city was in flames. United States heavy artillery had pounded the outskirts to rubble and now was beginning to fall on to the city center. The Seventh Californian, fresh from the Philippines, showed no mercy to their Mexican counterparts. Years of fighting the Moros had toughened their resolve and dissolved their conscience. Mexico City was a free fire zone.

General Pershing rode hard up to his cavalrymen.

"Those damn artillerymen are blowing everything to hell! Captain Washington!"

"Yes sir!"

"Get your men into the capital and collect as much intelligence as you can! I'll try to get those damn Californians to stop shelling our own men!" He rode of at a gallop towards the sound of the cannon.

"Eighth brigade, with me!" shouted Jesse. They rode

into the chaos of the city, shells screaming around them. The hooves of the horses clattered against the stone streets. They rode south of the closed United States Embassy and out down the Avenida de Independencia toward Calle de Lopez.

The road was bad, full of craters from the artillery. Most of the buildings were severely damaged and all of them had been evacuated. Each time they heard the scream of an artillery shell headed for the National Palace, they would spread out to minimize the casualties. The worst were the fragmentation shells. About thirty feet above their heads, they would explode, spreading shrapnel everywhere. Their tin hats protected them, but their horses had no such protection and those that survived bore many scars of warfare.

"Here!" Jesse yelled. He stood next to the shelled out German Imperial Embassy. "Get in and blow the safe! Bring me any papers you find in it!"

Lieutenant Little pulled up his horse next to Jesse. "Captain, that's German soil! There will be hell to pay if we get caught!"

Shells screamed overhead. "Little, do you see any

Germans?"

"No sir."

"Make sure it stays that way. Consider them open targets."

"Jesus Captain! Are you declaring war?"

"Just make sure there are no witnesses. Those German bastards have been supplying Mexico from the beginning. I want to know why!"

A muffled explosion came from within the building. Soldiers streamed out with armfuls of documents in their arms.

"Shove them in your saddle bags and let's get the hell out of here!"

The men jammed the papers into the leather bags. There was another muffled thump and then two more men ran out of the embassy.

"Captain, we blew the ambassadors safe, too. We've got everything that was in it!"

"Good work. Mount up!"

They troops rode hard for their own lines. The sound of the artillery grew louder. Finally, General Pershing's headquarters came into view. The troop pulled up, dismounted, and started unpacking their saddlebags. General Pershing strode out of his tent and grabbed a paper.

"Captain, this information is in German."

Jesse saluted. "Yes sir. The embassy was hit badly and these were all over the place. We just picked them up off the road."

"Pity that fine old building was destroyed."

"Mostly, sir."

"I see. Orderly!"

"Yes sir!"

Pershing quickly scrawled out a message. "Take this message to the captain of the artillery!"

The orderly saluted, shouted "Yes sir!" and ran off.

"Alright Captain, bring the papers into my tent."

"You heard the man. Diplomatic papers first!"

The soldiers began to bring in the haul of papers and stack them in a neat pile. Pershing began to sort through them. Washington stood at attention.

"Captain, scan these papers. Look for words you recognize like states."

Jesse sat at the table and began to sort through the papers. He didn't read German, but he had learned enough reading English to recognize common words.

"General, some of these papers are encoded. They're just numbers."

"Set them aside. Those are probably what we're after!"

After three hours, Pershing crowed, "We've got the code book! Let's look at those papers you set aside!"

They worked late into the night. Jesse would read the code and Pershing would look it up and write down the message. Around midnight, Pershing read the last message he had decoded.

"I need an official German translator."

An orderly ran out of the tent in search of a translator.

"Do we have it, General?"

"It would appear so, but I need to be sure."

The orderly returned with a sleepy soldier. "Sergeant Hesse speaks, reads, and writes fluent German."

Pershing handed him the paper. "Please let us know

what this paper says."

"It's a contract, between, the Government of the Republic of Mexico and, The Government of Imperial Germany. It's a list of armaments to be supplied by the Germans to the Mexicans in the event of war with the United States. The Germans will train Mexican troops, supply officer schools, and build armament factories. In exchange, Mexico will deliver Texas to the German empire as a North American colony. Mexico will be entitled to the United States territory west of the Rocky Mountains, including California. It's signed by President Madero and Kaiser Wilhelm II."

"This is the original. Could it be a fake?"

"It looks right." He held up the paper to the light, "See, Imperial watermark."

"Thank you, Sergeant. You are dismissed."

General Pershing looked at Captain Washington. "Who's left on the Mexican side?"

"General Zapata."

"Ask for a truce. He needs to see this."

Chapter 10

Mexico City, Mexico - September 1923

"You have asked for a truce. I don't see you surrendering. What is it you want, General Pershing?"

"We found some information near the German embassy that we wish to share with you." He handed General Zapata the decoded message.

"I do not read English. What is it?"

"An agreement between Madero and Kaiser Wilhelm to make war on the United States, dated 1912."

"What's your point?"

"We have both been manipulated by the Germans into this pointless war."

"Speak for yourself. We are defending our borders from Imperialist incursion."

"Which occurred after our borders were violated. Have you looked at your pistol?"

General Zapata slowly removed his Lugar. "What is

it you wish me to see?"

"It was made in the United States, for the Imperial German government. The CT stamping stands for Connecticut. Your first Mausers were from the same suppliers, before your factory in Tehuacán opened."

"The Germans are our allies."

"But the Americans are not, yet you carry American made pistols and rifles."

"What would you have me do? Regardless of the past, your troops shell the capitol and have captures large swaths of the north. My people will not stop until you withdraw from Mexico."

"General, we have lost over 40 million people in the United States to the war and the influenza. My intelligence places your population at less than seven million. We have added fresh troops from the Philippines. These are skilled warriors and will not hesitate to expand the war to your women and children. We have a chance to stop this. Let us agree on an armistice."

"The Californios? We have seen them in action. They do not follow the rules of war."

"I can only restrain them for so long, before President

Taft forces me to act."

"Your President Taft is old. He will not last another

term."

"Vice President Curtis is just as committed as

President Taft."

"I will consult with my Generals. Shall we meet

again tomorrow?"

"Yes, and we will hold the truce until after our

meeting."

"Bueno."

General Zapata left the meeting and rode back to his

troops. General Pershing spoke with Jesse on the way back

to their lines.

"What do you think?" Pershing asked.

"I think if he holds a square inch of Mexico, he'll

keep fighting for the rest."

"And if his army falls?"

"They'll fight in the fields and mountains."

"My opinion exactly. Do you know what Taft

wants?"

"No sir."

"To conquer and absorb Mexico."

"Is he crazy?"

"Imperialist. If we do that, we'll never have peace."

"He is our Commander in Chief."

"That he is, but if I can give him peace, he may back off."

"1913 borders?"

"I don't think the Mexicans will settle for less."

"All those people dead for a return to the status quo?"

"Not exactly. There are still the Germans to deal with."

"Helping the French could lead to war with the British."

"We could threaten to cut off munitions and loans to Britain if they interfered."

"If we did that to France, the war would be over."

"In Germany's favor. Would you reward them for what they did in North America?"

"Hell no!"

"Neither would I. Imagine if all the arms we've been

producing for Germany suddenly wound up in Russia."

"Germany could not stand up to them. They would lose."

"You're learning, Captain. There is more to winning wars than just winning battles on the ground."

The next day, talks with General Zapata continued.

"Good morning, General Zapata."

"Buenos dias, General Pershing."

"You've spoken with your generals?"

"Si, they are interested in what this armistice would look like."

"Return to the 1913 border, demilitarization of the states of both nations within 100 miles of the border between Mexico and the United States, and the repudiation of the Mexican - German alliance."

"Your government would agree to this?"

"It's an armistice, a military decision. The actual peace treaty would be hammered out by the politicians."

"They could reverse the entire armistice."

"Possibly, but not likely. What would your government do?"

"I am the acting Presidente. There is a lot of reformation needed in Mexico to prevent this from ever happening again."

"As we must in the United States, too. We will force the German defeat, with or without Mexico. That treaty is damning in its implications. With the armistice, your country can begin the healing process. Without it, we will push your army out of the Distrito Federal and all the way to the Yucatan."

"That could be harder than you think."

"I do not underestimate the professionalism and bravery of the Mexican army. Winning this war would be slaughter on a wholesale level. Both sides would scream in pain."

"That is sadly true. We will sign the armistice under the conditions you have presented."

"Upon signature, we will begin to withdraw from Mexico immediately."

Chapter 11

Vladivostok, U.S.S.R. April, 1925

Colonel Washington watched the ship from

California dock. As the gang plank lowered, he leapt up on it

and ran up to the deck.

"Permission to board!"

"Permission granted. Welcome aboard, Colonel."

"May I see the manifest, please?"

He took the papers and a large smile spread across

his face. "My Soviet counterpart will be very pleased!"

"Two hundred thousand Mausers with four million

rounds? He should be!"

"Any problems with the Germans?"

"We spotted a sub off Japan, but as we aren't at war

with Germany…"

"When these arms hit the Eastern Front, all hell is

going to break loose!"

"Now that Premier Kerensky has cleared out the

Imperial deadweight from command, their generals may actually speak to each other. There won't be a repeat of the Battle of Tannenberg. Generals Zhukov and Vasilevsky are young, but they are true military geniuses."

"What of the new land dreadnaughts?"

"The Soviets have vastly improved the French design. Henry Ford has done wonders with their assembly lines and quality control. When the Waco dreadnaughts strike, the Germans won't know what hit them."

"Waco?"

"In honor of the city in Texas. They also captured a nearly undamaged German Fokker D8 fighter. Their engineers have already improved it and have it in production. Did you see the British?"

"Off of Tokyo. They damn near gave us an escort to Vladivostok. Pershing must have put the fear of God in them."

"The Treasury put the fear of God in them. For now, they've backed off."

"How is President Pershing?"

"Busy. He's finished the treaty with Mexico."

"And?"

"Everyone is complaining."

"Uh oh."

"He tells me that's a good thing. It means everyone had to give up a little to get peace."

"What about Mexico?"

"They wanted reparations. They aren't getting them. That would have been a step too far for Congress. They had to settle for prewar borders and an open border in the north."

"Twelve years and no gains."

"I don't know. Zapata is a good President, segregation is dead, Diaz is gone, Madera is gone, the haciendas are being broken up, and trade between our countries has never been better."

"And Colt?"

"Broken up and sold off to their competitors. Their board is in prison convicted of war profiteering for selling Mauser and Lugar copies to the Germans. Those new guns come from Winchester and Smith and Wesson."

"Browning?"

"Their machine guns are in the new Waco

dreadnaughts. Fifty caliber and will shoot clean through a

brick wall."

"Where do you go from here?"

"With the guns you brought to the front as an advisor.

"God, be careful!"

"If the Mexicans couldn't kill me at Waco, the

Germans don't stand a chance!"

The End

www.ingramcontent.com/pod-product-compliance
Lightning Source LLC
Chambersburg PA
CBHW060447160726

47992CB00003B/1114